Luna And Her Two Big Wishes

Nelia F de Deus
Illustrated by Terri Kelleher

Thanks to: Suzan Spencer, Amna Haque and Gabby who helped with the editing.

Nelia F. de Deus© 2017
Illustrated by Terri Kelleher

Luna is a four-year-old girl who has two BIG WISHES. One is to be able to say HELLO to children of her own age, on her way to and from school or in the playing area. The other, is to have a BABY BROTHER.

On Luna's way to and from school, lots of things happen: people are rushing to and from work and rushing to and from school. Dads dropping children off, and mums picking them up. Mums dropping children off, and dads picking them up. Children walking alone or with their carer.

It is 8:30 am and the children start to arrive, one by one, two by two …
…until a large crowd forms.
Luna stands at the gate, feeling nervous and excited as she observes.
Lifting her head, she glances from the corner of her eye.
She notices some children chatting to each other. They all seem very
excited for the gate to be opened.

With a bright smile, here comes Mrs Smart.
"Good morning, children!"
"Good morning, Mrs Smart!" respond the children, very enthusiastically.

Seconds later they all disappear into the playground.
Everyone begins to interact with each other and play.
Feeling shy, Luna walks slowly, thinking this is her chance to say, HELLO.
Children are walking, skipping, running, jumping, playing, dancing, laughing, talking and sharing, and then sadly, the bell rings. No chance for Luna!

Although Luna feels shy, she is determined to say HELLO.
"I will try again tomorrow!" she thinks.
"I could have a go at lunch time!" she wonders.
Then, she remembers that each of the children already have their special
friend to sit with. However, Luna does not give up.
"I will say, HELLO today or tomorrow!" she decides.

Luna gets back home and tells her mum, Mrs Lorraine, that she didn't say HELLO to any children of her age on her way to and from school, or in the playing area.
"Don't worry Luna! Perhaps, some children were running late, and rushing to get to school on time."
"Let's set the alarm so we can walk with those who are not too early or late," reassures her mum.

The next morning when the alarm goes off, Luna wakes immediately. She dresses herself and goes down to the front door.
"Mummy! I'm ready! Let's go!" she calls out excitedly.

On the way, Luna notices a little boy, who she recognises from the playground the day before. She touches his arm, hoping that he remembers her.

"Mummy! Did you notice?" Luna yells.

"No," answers Mrs Lorraine.

"I just touched a little boy's arm," she says.

"What happened, Luna?"

"Nothing…nothing," she pauses sadly.

"I thought he would remember me! I saw him in the playground yesterday, holding his sister's hand."

"Don't worry Luna, keep calm. You will make a friend and have a chance to say HELLO very soon!" comforts Mrs Lorraine.

People are rushing to and from work, and rushing to and from school. Dads dropping children off, and mums picking them up. Mums dropping children off, and dads picking them up. Children are walking alone or with their carer.

Luna stands again outside the gate with her mum, hoping that she will have a chance to say, HELLO. Then, Mrs Smart spots her and says:
"Good morning, Luna!"
Alongside the other children, Luna answers:
"Good morning, Mrs Smart!"
Luna is not only being seen by Mrs Smart, but by everyone surrounding her.
Soon after, boys and girls approach her and ask for her name.
"Will you play with me?"
"Would you like to join us?"
"Let's play teachers!"
"Who wants to be the student?" asks Luna confidently.
Luna feels amazing, being called to join in and take part.

It's lunch time, and Luna doesn't know where to sit. Then, there are lots of invitations:
"Here Luna," calls one.
"With me Luna, please, please!" demands another.
"This side Luna!" shouts someone from the other side of the table.
Luna feels very welcome.
The children play a game and say, "Whoever wins can sit next to her."
Luna becomes a very happy girl.

On her way to school, Luna greets the children with a great big smile …
… *In the playground: walking, skipping, running, jumping, playing, dancing, laughing, talking and sharing …*
In the classroom: listening, learning and willing to take part.
"My first dream has just come true!" concludes Luna.
"Thank you Mummy, you have supported me!" she says to herself.

The following day, Luna wakes up feeling that something is missing, and she asks;
"Mummy, can I have a BABY BROTHER?"
"Of course, you can! We can buy one," suggests Mrs Lorraine.
"Can you buy it for my birthday?"
"Yes, I will … from a pet shop!"
"A pet shop? MY BABY BROTHER from a pet shop?"
Luna is a bit confused.
"Sure," smiles Mrs Lorraine.

Later that day, Mrs Lorraine takes Luna to the pet shop.
"Here Luna, you can see lots of BABY PETS from which you can choose one to buy."
"It could be: a BABY HAMSTER, a BABY GUINEA PIG, a BABY FISH, a BABY BUDGIE, a KITTEN, or a BABY RABBIT…"
"Can we get it now? Please Mummy!"
"Not yet Luna, but soon! I need to find a cosy place for it."
"In my room, it can sleep in my bed!" insists Luna.
"But, where are you going to sleep, Luna?"
"On the floor, Mummy! On the floor. Please, please, Mummy!"
Mrs Lorraine tells Luna, "Not only does a BABY need a room, but somebody to look after them every day."
"Me, me, me, Mummy! You, you, you! Me, you, you, me! Me, you!"

"See Luna, it ends with me! I don't have any spare time," says Mrs Lorraine.

"Mummy … if I do all the things you ask me to do, can you buy a REAL BABY like me, when I was very little? Please Mummy!"
"Which things, Luna?"
"Wash my hands after the toilet … one."
"Don't jump on the bed … two."
"Don't scream … three."
"Don't run away when it's bath-time … four."
"Eat all my food, including my vegetables … five."
"Drink my water… six."
"Don't ask to buy everything from the toy shop … seven."
"There is more though," she continues, "like … watching too much TV? It could be eight! Things like that … please Mummy!"
"That's a good list Luna. I will think about it," says Mrs Lorraine.

Next day at play, Luna tells the children that her mum is going to buy her a BABY BROTHER.
"Buying a BABY? YOUR BROTHER? I don't believe it!" says one of the children. "You can't buy a BABY, a real BABY!"
Luna becomes very sad. She thinks she's going to get a BABY that will be just like her, when she was very little.
At the end of the school day, Luna walks quietly. So, her mum asks: "How was your day, Luna?"
Luna doesn't reply.
Mrs Lorraine goes home via the pet shop, to surprise Luna.

At the pet shop, Mrs Lorraine asks Luna which pet she would like to have. Without any hesitation, she answers:
"A BABY HAMSTER! The white one … she's called Rosie."
At home, Mum and daughter are very happy with the arrival of BABY Rosie.
Back at school, no one asks Luna about the baby she's getting.
Luna cares so much about Rosie that she considers her as a family member. Luna only achieves one of her TWO BIG WISHES. In her mind, she still wants a BABY BROTHER, yet she's happy with BABY Rosie.
"A good sister."

Now try these verbs. If you know them, just give it a tick, if not, look it up in a dictionary.

Insist	☐	Arrive	☑
Rush	☑	Suggest	☐
Drop	☑	Wonder	☑
Observe	☐	Buy	☑
Remember	☑	Support	☐
Approach	☐	Reassure	☐

Here are some questions to test your knowledge.

1. What happened when Luna didn't know where to sit?
2. How did Luna feel after Mrs Smart spotted her?
3. How many promises did Luna make to her mum, if she bought her a REAL BABY?
4. What colour is Luna's hamster?

Here is another book by the same Author.
Hermia Can't Sleep.
Available on Amazon.

19879831R00024

Printed in Poland
by Amazon Fulfillment
Poland Sp. z o.o., Wrocław